HEIDI HECKELBECK

and the Magic Puppy

By Wanda Coven
Illustrated by Priscilla Burris

LITTLE SIMON
New York London Toronto Sydney New Delhi

LITTLE SIMON
An imprint of Simon & Schuster Children's Publishing Division
1230 Avenue of the Americas, New York, New York 10020
First Little Simon hardcover edition June 2017
Copyright © 2017 by Simon & Schuster, Inc.
Also available in a Little Simon paperback edition.
All rights reserved, including the right of reproduction in whole or in part in any form. LITTLE SIMON is a registered trademark of Simon & Schuster, Inc., and associated colophon is a trademark of Simon & Schuster, Inc. For information about special discounts for bulk purchases, please contact Simon & Schuster Special Sales at 1-866-506-1949 or business@simonandschuster.com. The Simon & Schuster Speakers Bureau can bring authors to your live event. For more information or to book an event contact the Simon & Schuster Speakers Bureau at 1-866-248-3049 or visit our website at www.simonspeakers.com.
Designed by Ciara Gay
Manufactured in the United States of America 0517 FFG
10 9 8 7 6 5 4 3 2 1
Library of Congress Cataloging-in-Publication Data
Names: Coven, Wanda, author. | Burris, Priscilla, illustrator.
Title: Heidi Heckelbeck and the magic puppy / by Wanda Coven ; illustrated by Priscilla Burris.
Description: First Little Simon paperback edition. | New York : Little Simon, 2017. | Series: Heidi Heckelbeck ; 20 | Summary: Unable to find the owners of a lost puppy, Heidi decides to use just a teensy-weensy pinch of magic that sets off a mega-gigantic case of magic puppy trouble.
Identifiers: LCCN 2016034665 | ISBN 9781481495219 (pbk) | ISBN 9781481495226 (hc) | ISBN 9781481495233 (eBook)
Subjects: | CYAC: Dogs—Fiction. | Animals—Infancy—Fiction. | Lost and found possessions—Fiction. | Magic—Fiction. | Witches—Fiction.
Classification: LCC PZ7.C83393 Hbm 2017 | DDC [Fic]—dc23
LC record available at https://lccn.loc.gov/2016034665

CONTENTS

A Day at the Park

Skippity skip!

Hoppity hop!

Jumpity jump!

Heidi Heckelbeck, Lucy Lancaster, and Bruce Bickerson pranced along the path through Charmed Court Park. Bruce twirled a white Frisbee on the end of his pointer finger. Lucy hopped out of the way of two roller-bladers. Heidi stopped and pointed to a yoga class on the lawn.

"Let's see if we can do some of their poses!" she suggested.

They watched the yoga instructor. Lucy bent over into a dolphin pose.

Bruce wove himself into an eagle
pose. And Heidi struck a lord of the
dance pose. Then they dropped to the
ground, laughing.

"Now let's play on the giant chess-board!" Lucy said, taking off. Heidi and Bruce followed close behind. They played hide-and-seek among the oversize chess pieces. Then they

ran to the playground, slid down the slides, and swung on the monkey bars.

"Let's ride the zip line!" cried Heidi.

Heidi climbed the ladder that led

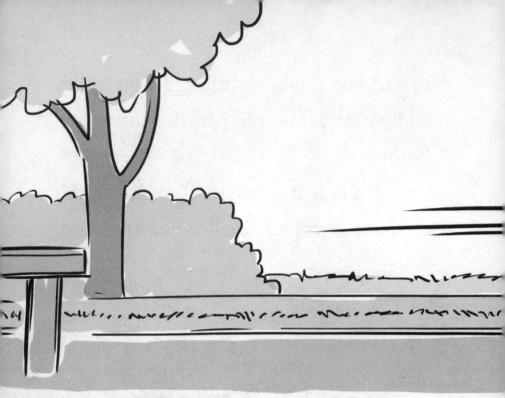

up to the wooden platform. Then she
grabbed the cable and hopped onto
the seat. The wire made a pleasing
hum as she sailed through the air.
She stuck out her feet, scrunched her
knees, and pushed off the platform

at the other end of the zip line, and
away she went. Then Lucy and Bruce
each had a turn.

Heidi waited and watched a boy
fly an orange dragon kite. She could
also see picnickers on blankets in the

shade of the trees. Bicyclists, joggers, and skateboarders paraded down the path. *I love the park,* she thought.

Bruce zip-lined to the ground with a thud and picked up his disc. "Okay, can we please play Frisbee now?" he said, leading the girls to a grassy area.

They spread out in a triangle. Bruce curled his wrist and snapped the Frisbee. The disc flew straight to Heidi's open hand. Heidi gripped the Frisbee and threw it to Lucy— only the disc swerved away from her friend. Lucy ran after it, caught it, and hurled it to Bruce. This time

Bruce snapped a fancy backhander. The Frisbee soared way up in the air and then swooped down into the bushes. Heidi went after it.

She bent over and peered into the foliage. Then she jumped back suddenly and fell on her bottom. "Aaaaah!" she screamed.

The Frisbee had jumped out of the bush all by itself. Well, not exactly all by itself. . . .

"Whoa!" Heidi cried. "Take a look at THIS! It's a puppy!"

Chapter 2

PUPPY LOVE

The puppy had a short, but shaggy brown coat with skinny legs. His tiny eyes stared back at them, and his ears stood out like two floppy handlebars. The puppy had the Frisbee in his mouth. Heidi held out her hand. The puppy went down on his front paws, sending his fluffy hind quarters and little tail up in the air. He growled playfully.

Lucy and Bruce ran over and kneeled beside Heidi. Bruce grabbed ahold of his Frisbee and tugged it out of the puppy's mouth.

"Yip! Yap!" the puppy barked.

Bruce inspected the surface of his Frisbee. "Hey, you got TEETH marks on it!" he scolded.

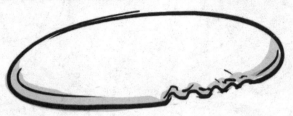

"Yip! Yap!" the puppy responded.

Heidi shook her head. "Isn't he SO cute?" she said, ignoring the damage to the Frisbee.

Bruce frowned. "Teeth marks are NOT cute," he said. "I bought this Frisbee with my own money, you know."

Lucy looked at the Frisbee. "You can barely tell," she said.

Bruce sighed.

"You have to admit, this puppy IS adorable," Heidi repeated. "Even his

little teeth chomps in your Frisbee
are cute!"

Lucy laughed. "He is pretty adorable," she said.

"And destructive,"
Bruce added.

Heidi ruffled the
puppy's fur. Then
she looked at its
collar. "Hey," she
said. "This puppy
doesn't have a
tag. Hmm, I won-
der if the puppy
is lost?"

All three of them looked around.
There didn't seem to be anyone
nearby.

"Maybe we should try to find the owner," Heidi suggested.

The puppy barked and wagged his short, pointy tail.

"I think we have ourselves a new mission!" declared Lucy.

So they set off in search of the owner. The puppy followed Bruce because he had the Frisbee.

First they went to the dog park.

"Do you know the owner of this puppy?" Heidi asked a gray-haired man throwing a ball for his Labradoodle.

"Sorry," the man said as his dog raced after the ball. "I've never seen that cute little guy before."

Then they asked a lady wearing a skirt with daisies on it and a guy

who was surrounded by tiny dogs
that barked. No one knew this puppy
or his owner. After the dog park they
asked everyone at the picnic grounds
and in the playground area. Nobody

seemed to know anything about the lost puppy.

"Now what?" asked Heidi.

Lucy petted the puppy's head. "You know, most dogs have microchips nowadays," she said. "Maybe a vet can track down the owner."

"Frankie's vet is right on the edge of the park," Bruce said, pointing to one of the park entrances. Bruce had a dog named Benjamin Franklin. He called him Frankie for short.

"What are we waiting for?" Heidi said. "Let's go!"

Bruce took off his belt and attached it to the puppy's collar to create a makeshift leash. Then—*"Yip! Yip! Yip! Yip!"*—they walked to the vet.

Chapter 3

A PET OF MY OWN

Bruce led the puppy to the front desk at the vet's office. "We found a puppy at the park," Bruce began.

Heidi shook her head. "No, no, no—the puppy found US," she corrected him.

The receptionist raised one of her

thin eyebrows. "Is the puppy lost?" she asked.

All three children nodded.

"We'd like to see if the puppy has a microchip," Lucy said. "We're trying to find the owner."

Heidi picked up the puppy and showed the receptionist.

"Do you like the puppy's leash?" Heidi asked. "It's a belt."

The receptionist smiled. "That's very clever," she said. "Please have a seat. I'll call when the doctor's ready."

The waiting room was crowded. Heidi, Lucy, and Bruce had to sit

separately. Bruce sat with the puppy.
Heidi looked at the lady next to her.
She had a golden retriever. The girl on
the other side of her had a guinea pig.

It had the name
Mulch   written
on the carrier.
Then the man
across   from
her had a big
birdcage with
a red parrot
inside, but the
man didn't look
like a pirate.

Heidi wanted to
see all the animals, so
she got up and walked around the
waiting room. She met a chinchilla, a

turtle, and three cats. She also learned that Brodie, the golden retriever, had eaten an entire birthday cake.

All these pets made Heidi long for a pet too. She kneeled beside the puppy and rubbed the fringe above his eyes. *Maybe you can be MY puppy,* she thought.

"It's your turn, lost puppy," called the receptionist.

Bruce and Lucy jumped to their feet. Heidi sighed and hugged the dog. "I hope you don't have an owner," she whispered in the puppy's ear.

Then they followed the reception-ist to a room in the back. The vet had on a lab coat and white rubber gloves. Bruce set the puppy on the metal table.

The vet held the puppy gently but firmly. "What a cute pup!" she said.

She waved something over the scruff of the puppy's neck. "This is a scanner. It beeps if there's a microchip," said the vet. But it didn't beep.

"Well, I'm afraid this guy isn't chipped," she said. "I would be happy to take him to the animal shelter after work—that's where most owners look for lost pets."

The puppy barked sharply. He didn't seem to like that idea. Neither did Heidi. She scooped him up and held him close.

"Thanks for the offer," Heidi said, trying to sound agreeable. "We'll take it from here."

Then she headed toward the door. Lucy and Bruce followed her, but not before looking at each other with wide eyes as if to say, *What is that crazy girl up to NOW?*

Chapter 4

GIVE ME A SIGN

Once they were back outside, Lucy and Bruce surrounded Heidi and held out their arms to stop her.

"Heidi?" asked Lucy. "Why didn't you let the vet take the puppy?"

Heidi pushed past them and kept walking. "How was I supposed to let this POOR little puppy go to a shelter?" she cried. "What if he gets kennel cough or—worse—gets scared by a huge, mean dog?"

"Or gets picked up by his OWNER!" Bruce pointed out as he caught up to his friend.

Heidi stooped down and nuzzled
the puppy. "I have a better idea," she
said, putting on the leash. "Let's make
Found Puppy signs and hang them
up around the neighborhood."

Lucy and Bruce looked at each other.

"Come on, guys, please? The puppy can stay at my house while we hang up the signs," Heidi added. She stared longingly at her friends.

"Okay," Lucy agreed. "But I'm doing it for the puppy—not you."

"Me too," Bruce agreed.

Heidi hopped for joy.

"Watch out, Heidi," Lucy warned. "You're falling for this puppy."

Heidi pointed to her-self and pretended to look shocked. "Who, me?" she said innocently.

"Yes, YOU!" Lucy and Bruce said at the same time.

Heidi shrugged like it was no big deal. Then they headed for her house.

★ ✲ ✳ ◎ ★

"MOM!" Heidi shouted as soon as they tramped in the back door. "YOU'LL NEVER GUESS WHAT!"

Mom and Henry walked into the kitchen.

"We found a lost PUPPY!"

Henry ran straight for the furry visitor. "He's so CUTE!"

The puppy licked Henry on the nose. Mom folded her arms and shook her head.

"Don't worry!" Heidi said. "We are going to make lots of Found Puppy posters. Then we'll put them ALL over the neighborhood!"

Mom tapped her foot. "And if that doesn't work?" she questioned.

"Then we will KEEP HIM!" Heidi suggested.

Henry pumped his fists. "YES!" he cried.

"I am afraid not," said Dad as he walked into the room from his lab. "Maybe we will get a pet some-day, but today is not that day. You'll need to find the owner or take him to the shelter. I'll bet someone is look-ing for this little pup."

Heidi didn't want to think about that, so she raced off with her friends to gather art supplies. They pulled out all the paper and markers they could find. Bruce took a picture of the puppy, and Dad printed several

copies on his printer. Then they sat
around the table and made signs:

FOUND!
Do you know this puppy?

Found at
Charmed Court Park.
Please call: (503) ear-deol

Heidi also made a
secret sign for herself:

FOUND!
Do you know this puppy?

Because he's awesome!
Please don't call!
I'm serious.

Chapter 5

UH-OH!

Heidi carefully set a bowl of water on the floor. Her mom had made a safe place in the kitchen so the puppy wouldn't get into any trouble while everyone was out hanging flyers.

"You are a GOOD puppy, aren't you? Yes, you are!" she said, petting the dog's head. "You would never get in trouble, would you, boy?"

The puppy cocked his head at her and raised one ear. He knew something was going on.

"Don't worry. We'll be back soon," she reassured him. Then she whispered, "And hopefully nobody will claim you, and you'll be ALL MINE!"

Heidi, her family, and Lucy and Bruce hung the Found Puppy signs everywhere. They tacked them on telephone poles throughout the neighborhood. They posted them at all the entrances to the park. They

even put signs up in the local coffee shop and at Scoops. Everyone got ice cream for the walk home.

"*Yip! Yap! Yip!*" Heidi could hear the puppy barking and scratching at the back door.

"It sounds like the puppy missed me!" she said over her shoulder to Lucy and Bruce.

Then Heidi

opened the door and gasped. "Oh no!" she cried, covering her mouth with her hand.

"What's the matter?" Lucy asked. She peeked inside the door too. Then, just like Heidi, she drew in a great breath. "Uh-oh," she said.

Bruce stood on tiptoe and peered inside. "Oh, wow!" he said.

Henry squeezed in between them. "Oh, double wow," he said. Then he turned to his sister. "You're in BIG trouble."

Mr. and Mrs. Heckelbeck were the last to walk up the steps.

"What's going on?" Mom asked.

The children silently stepped out of the way. Heidi's parents walked in the door.

"MY HOUSE!" cried Heidi's mom. "IT'S A MESS!"

The puppy barked happily. Dad quickly grabbed the puppy and handed him to Bruce. "Can you and Lucy please take the puppy into the backyard?" he said.

"Heidi and Henry, you help us clean up."

Heidi looked around the kitchen. She didn't know where to begin.

All the kitchen towels had been pulled out of the drawers. A bag of chewed pretzels lay on the ground. A

box of cereal had toppled over and
scattered everywhere. All the new
seat cushions had been tugged off
the chairs, and the stuffing had been

completely pulled out of one. Clumps of fluff skittered around the floor.

"Watch out for the puddle of PEE!" Henry called, pointing.

Mom let out a long "Oh . . . my . . . goodness."

"Don't worry. I'll get it," Dad offered, grabbing a roll of paper towels.

Heidi walked into the pantry to get a broom. A trail of uncooked tortellini crunched under her feet. She stared at the floor. Everything from the first shelf had been pulled out and torn open. She grabbed the broom.

"OH NO-NO!" Henry called. "Dad! It looks like the puppy broke into your lab, too!"

Dad dropped the paper towels and race downstairs. Mom followed after him. Heidi heard more cries and howls from the lab.

How could one little puppy cause so much damage? she wondered. She frowned. *Now Mom and Dad will never let me keep him!* Then she had another disturbing thought. *If I don't find the owner, that poor puppy WILL wind up in a shelter!*

Somebody knocked on the back door. Heidi leaned the broom against the wall and ran to the door. Lucy held out the puppy for Heidi.

"Sorry to leave you like this, but my mom's here," Lucy said. "Bruce and I have to go."

Heidi took the puppy in her arms. He licked Heidi's face. "Okay, I'll see you later," Heidi said.

Once she was alone, Heidi looked in the puppy's playful eyes. "What am I going to do with you?" she asked him.

Then Heidi had an idea.

Chapter 6

MERG-A-LAT;ON!

Heidi raced to her room with the puppy in her arms. Once inside, she closed the door, set him down, and reached under her bed to pull out her *Book of Spells*. Heidi scanned the Contents page for a lost-and-found spell and put her finger right on one.

The Lost-and-Found Spell

Have you ever lost something dear to you? A piece of jewelry? A pair of glasses? A pet? Or perhaps the trouble is the other way around. Have you ever found a piece of jewelry, a pair of glasses, or a pet? Maybe you are the kind of witch who likes to find or restore lost items? Then this is the spell for you!

Ingredients:

1 map that includes the area in which the item was lost or found

1 handful of dirt

2 leaves, crumpled

4 sour gummy worms

1 picture of what is lost or found

Mix all the ingredients together in a bowl, except the picture of the lost or found item. Then hold your Witches of Westwick medallion in one hand and hold the picture over the mix with your other hand. Chant the following spell:

HELP RESTORE
MY PEACE OF MIND.
LEAD ME TO WHAT I NEED TO FIND.
BE IT LOST OR BE IT FOUND,
BRING IT BACK
SAFE AND SOUND.

Heidi quickly gathered the spell ingredients in a bowl and stirred the mix. The puppy watched closely. Heidi clutched her medallion in one hand and held the picture of the puppy over the mix in the other. She began to chant the spell.

"Yip! Yap!" The little dog barked right in the middle of her chant.

"Shhh!" Heidi shushed as she continued the spell.

Then the puppy leaped into her lap. *Ker-splat!* The ingredients flew *everywhere*!

"Oh, MERG!" yelled Heidi, scooping everything back into the bowl.

The puppy scampered under the bed. Heidi lay on her stomach and helped the puppy back out. Dirt from the spell was now all over Heidi, the puppy, and her room.

"Oh, MERG-A-LATION!" Heidi cried. "Now the spell is RUINED—AND everything is covered in dirt!"

Heidi's whole day needed a do-over, but this crazy puppy needed a bath.

Chapter 7

GO, DOG! GO!

Heidi filled the tub partway with water. Then she placed the wriggly puppy in the tub and squirted some shampoo onto his back. He relaxed as she lathered his fur.

"No dirty pups in THIS house!" she told him.

Then Heidi noticed something odd out of the corner of her eye. She slowly turned her head and let out a yelp. Her toilet had turned into a FIRE HYDRANT. She looked back at the puppy.

"Arf!" he barked playfully.

Then Heidi heard a splashing sound. All the tub toys had come to life. A rubber duck quacked and swam on its own. A tiny scuba person splashed in the water. *Oh my gosh,* Heidi thought. *What's going on?*

She lost her grip
on the sudsy puppy.
He leaped out of the
tub and ran into her room.
Heidi jumped up to chase him. She
found the wet dog on her bed . . .
only, it wasn't her bed anymore. It
had turned into a giant DOG bed! And
her stuffed animals had all turned
into CHEW toys!

"Oh no!" Heidi cried. "The spell has gone haywire!"

All of a sudden, the tiny puppy floated off the ground! He flew past Heidi and out of the bedroom.

She thundered downstairs after him. Everything in the house had turned into dog supplies. All the furniture had become giant dog toys. The chairs had turned into huge shoes— the grown-up kinds that puppies love to chew on. Even the fireplace had changed—into a doghouse.

Heidi dashed into the kitchen. The
table had turned into a gigantic bone,
and the magic puppy happily gnawed
on it.

Heidi looked at the open cup-
boards. All the food had turned into
DOG food. And all of Mom's fine
china had been replaced by
dog bowls. This was big-time
puppy trouble! Heidi grabbed

the phone and hit speed dial. "Pick up! PICK UP!" she pleaded.

"Hello?" There was a cheery voice on the other end of the line.

"AUNT TRUDY!" Heidi shouted into the phone. "It's me, HEIDI! Help! I have a Heidi-mergency, if you know what I mean! Please come right away!"

Her Aunt Trudy did not ask any questions. "I'm on my way!" she said.

Chapter 8

VAMOOSE!

Aunt Trudy arrived before Heidi had even hung up.

"How did you DO that?" Heidi asked with a startled jump.

"Tell you later," Aunt Trudy said, looking around. "What's going on?" she asked.

Heidi bit her lip and explained everything.

"And then the puppy jumped into the mix—right when I was casting the spell!"

Aunt Trudy nodded thoughtfully. "The magic went straight to the puppy," she said. "But this sure is a *lot* of magic. I wonder if this puppy was already enchanted."

Heidi shook her head. "I don't think so," she said.

Aunt Trudy looked around. "Where is everybody?" she asked.

Heidi pointed at her dad's lab.

"They're cleaning up another mess the puppy made," she said. "Do you think we can fix this disaster before they're done?"

Aunt Trudy nodded. Then she began

to chant a spell: "Shoo wa ditty ditty dum ditty dee! Reverse this puppy spell on the count of three. One! Two! Three!"

Aunt Trudy waved her hand, and a great gust of magical sparkles swirled all through the whole house. *Zap!* Everything was returned to normal—even the water had disappeared from the puppy's fur.

Then Henry came bursting into the kitchen from the laboratory.

"We're done!" he said triumphantly. "Wow! Are you finished cleaning in here?"

Heidi shrugged. "Yup," she said. "Aunt Trudy helped me."

Then Mom and Dad walked into the kitchen.

neighborhood and recognized your phone number. I just had to meet this sweet puppy you found."

Dad rolled his eyes. "I wouldn't exactly call him sweet," he said.

"Yeah, more like destructive," Henry added. "Where is that guy, anyway?"

The family looked at the wide-open back door.

"Oh no!" Heidi howled. "I think the puppy ESCAPED!"

"Hi, Trudy," Mom said. "When did you get here?"

"A little while ago," she said, pulling a Found Puppy poster from her pocket. "I saw this sign in the

Chapter 9

GET A CLUE!

"We have to rescue the puppy!" Heidi cried. "What if the owners call? Or worse—what if the puppy gets picked up by Animal Control?"

Henry grabbed a rope from his backpack. "We can use this rope to capture him," he offered.

75

Dad sighed and jammed on a baseball cap. "All right, gang. Let's finish what we started," he said, heading for the door. Everyone followed.

"So, how DO we find the puppy?" asked Henry as he looked up and down the street.

"We have to look for clues," Heidi

said. She inspected a fire hydrant beside the sidewalk. "See? It's wet," she said. "That means the puppy probably marked it. Let's go this way."

Henry bent over and looked at the hydrant. "Wow," he said. "You're a good detective."

Mom, Dad, and Aunt Trudy spread out and looked for clues too.

Then Detective Heidi noticed a dug-up garden. "Broken tulip stems," she observed. "And notice how the dirt has been kicked onto the grass."

Henry studied the garden too. "We're definitely on the right track."

They ran down the sidewalk in search of more clues. The grown-ups trailed behind. Henry pointed to a garden hose spurting a fountain of water.

"There's a hole in that hose!" he shouted. "Could the puppy have done it?"

Heidi ran onto the lawn and picked up the hose. As she

inspected it, water sprayed all over her.

"I'd know those cute little teeth marks anywhere!" she declared, wiping the water from her face with the back of her hand.

"Aha!" Henry cried. "We're still hot on the puppy's trail!"

Heidi noticed the park entrance up ahead and cheered. "I've solved this puppy mystery! To the park!"

Heidi and Henry ran to the corner and pushed the cross-walk signal. Mom, Dad, and Aunt Trudy caught up by the time the light changed. Heidi explained that she thought the puppy might have gone back to the park. "I'll show

you where we found him in the first place," Heidi said, leading the way.

Everyone followed Heidi to the grassy spot where they had been playing Frisbee. Heidi kneeled beside the bushes and pulled apart the branches. The bush began to tremble, and the puppy pounced from his hiding place.

"Awwww!" Heidi cried. "We found you!" Then she hugged him as if *she* were the puppy's long-lost owner.

Chapter 10

WiZARD

"Can we keep him?" Heidi asked her parents. "Please?"

Her parents shook their heads.

"He isn't ours," Mom said. "And for another thing, the puppy almost destroyed our house in two hours!"

"That's right. Can you imagine if we

had him for a full day?" added Dad.

Heidi and Henry both turned on
their own sad, puppy-dog eyes.

Aunt Trudy laughed.

"But he NEEDS us," Heidi said, pick-
ing up a stick and dangling it in front

of the puppy. The puppy clamped his teeth on the stick and pulled. A tug-of-war followed.

"*No,*" said Mom and Dad firmly.

"But we could train him!" Henry argued.

"No," they said again.

Then Mom's phone rang. Everyone froze. They all listened as Mom checked the number and answered the call.

"Hello? Yes?" she said. "Oh, really? Uh-huh. Oh, we're in Charmed Court Park now. You're welcome. Yes, we'll be right over."

Heidi and Henry slumped into a heap on the grass.

"The owners?" Heidi asked as the puppy climbed into her lap.

Mom nodded. "Actually, they live right around the corner," she said.

Heidi hugged the puppy and let out

a heavy sigh. Henry hung his head.

"I guess we have to take him back to his rightful owners," Heidi said.

Mom, Dad, and Aunt Trudy all nodded this time.

★ ✦ ✳ ◎ ✦

The house looked like a fairy-tale cottage. It had a foundation made of stones and a little turret roof. The gray-blue shutters matched the gray-blue front door, and all the windows

had window boxes filled with flowers
spilling over the sides.

Heidi and Henry climbed the steps
to the stoop and knocked on the door.
Aunt Trudy followed. Heidi's parents

waited at the edge of the sidewalk.
The door unlatched and clicked open.

Heidi's and Henry's eyes grew very
wide.

"What? Principal Pennypacker?"
Heidi said in surprise.

He smiled and nodded warmly.
"Hello, Heidi and Henry!" he said as
if he was expecting them.

The principal had on shorts and a polo shirt—not a suit like he usually wore to school. A little girl with blond hair peeked out from behind him.

"WIZARD!" she cried happily when she saw the puppy. Heidi let go of the dog, and he ran to the little girl. She held him close. "I thought I'd lost you FOREVER!"

The puppy licked her cheeks and happily wagged his tail.

"This is my niece, Anna," said Principal Pennypacker. "She is visiting and just got Wizard a few days ago. He's quite a little rascal and keeps sneaking away."

Heidi and Aunt Trudy laughed.

"Well, Wizard is a perfect name for him," Aunt Trudy said.

Principal Pennypacker shook his head. "You're not kidding," he said. "He's like having a furry toddler with magical powers."

Heidi and Aunt Trudy looked at each other in surprise. It seemed odd that the principal would use the word "magical" to describe the puppy after the crazy day they'd had.

"Thank you for making the signs," Anna said. "We never would have found Wizard without your help. He

didn't have his dog tag on because he'd pulled it off!"

Anna kneeled down and attached Wizard's missing dog tag.

Heidi did a double take when she saw it. *Whoa,* she thought. *Wizard's dog tag looks like a miniature version of my Witches of Westwick medallion!*

"Yes, well, thank you, Heidi," said

Principal Pennypacker. "And thank you, Henry. And the rest of the Heckelbeck family too! We really appreciate what you've done for us."

Heidi forced herself to stop staring at the puzzling dog tag. *Maybe it's just a weird coincidence,* she thought. But she wasn't sure.

She nuzzled Wizard one last time, and even though she wished he were *her* puppy, she was very happy that Wizard was

finally back with his proper family.

"Good-bye, Anna," she said. "Good-bye, Wizard."

Then she caught Aunt Trudy's eye on the way out the door. Had she noticed the dog tag too?

Hmm, Heidi thought. *Very mysterious. Very mysterious indeed.* And she could tell that her aunt was thinking the exact same thing.

"Are you going to be okay without Wizard, Heidi?" Aunt Trudy asked.

"Definitely," Heidi said with a smile. "Something tells me Wizard is exactly where he belongs."